Welcome to ALADDIN QUIX

If you are looking for fast, fun-to read stories with colorful characters, lots of kid-friendly humor, easy-to-follow action, entertaining story lines, and lively illustrations, then **ALADDIN QUIX** is for you!

But wait, there's more!

If you're also looking for stories with tables of contents; word lists; about-the-book questions; 64, 80, or 96 pages; short chapters; short paragraphs; and large fonts, then **ALADDIN QUIX** is *definitely* for you!

ALADDIN QUIX: The next step between ready to reads and longer, more challenging chapter books, for readers five to eight years old.

FIELD TRIP

**Read more ALADDIN QUIX books
featuring Geeger!**

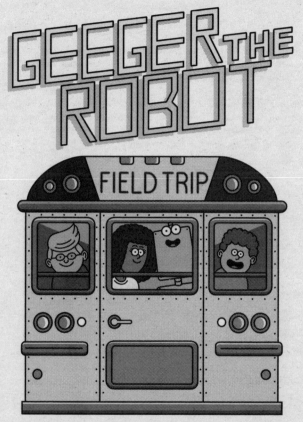

GEEGER THE ROBOT

FIELD TRIP

BY
**Jarrett
Lerner**

ILLUSTRATED
BY
**Serge
Seidlitz**

ALADDIN QUIX

New York London Toronto Sydney New Delhi

ALADDIN QUIX
Simon & Schuster Children's Publishing Division
1230 Avenue of the Americas, New York, New York 10020
First Aladdin QUIX paperback edition September 2023
Text copyright © 2023 by Jarrett Lerner
Illustrations copyright © 2023 by Serge Seidlitz
Also available in an Aladdin QUIX hardcover edition.
All rights reserved, including the right of reproduction in whole or in part in any form.
ALADDIN and the related marks and colophon are
trademarks of Simon & Schuster, Inc.
For information about special discounts for bulk purchases, please contact
Simon & Schuster Special Sales at 1-866-506-1949 or business@simonandschuster.com.
The Simon & Schuster Speakers Bureau can bring authors to your live event.
For more information or to book an event contact the Simon & Schuster Speakers Bureau
at 1-866-248-3049 or visit our website at www.simonspeakers.com.
Series designed by Karin Paprocki
Cover designed by Ginny Kemmerer
Interior designed by Mike Rosamilia
The illustrations for this book were rendered digitally.
The text of this book was set in Archer Medium.
Manufactured in the United States of America 0723 OFF
2 4 6 8 10 9 7 5 3 1
Library of Congress Control Number 2023933129
ISBN 9781665910934 (hc)
ISBN 9781665910927 (pbk)
ISBN 9781665910941 (ebook)

For Serge

Cast of Characters

Geeger: A very, very hungry robot

DIGEST-O-TRON 5000: A machine that turns the food Geeger eats into electricity

Ms. Bork: Geeger's teacher

Tillie: A student at Geeger's school, and Geeger's best friend

Arjun, Olivia, Mac, Sidney, Suzie, Gabe, Roxy, Raul: Other kids in Geeger's class, and also Geeger's friends

Fudge: Ms. Bork's class pet hamster

Albert Einstein: Tillie's dog

Chef Mike: The chef at Geeger's school

Contents

A Hero!

Geeger is a robot. A very, very hungry robot.

Geeger was built by a team of scientists, then sent to work in a town called Amblerville.

Geeger is good at his job. Really,

really, really, really, **REALLY** good.

That's because Geeger's job is to EAT—and eating might be the thing that Geeger is best at.

But Geeger doesn't eat just anything. No, no, no. Geeger eats all the food that the people of Amblerville don't want to eat themselves.

Like slices of bread that are so moldy, they're more *green* than bread-colored.

Like hunks of cheese so old and stinky, even *flies* won't get anywhere near them.

Like pieces of fruit so rotten, it's hard to tell what they even are. An apple? An orange? An avocado? A pear? Who knows! Geeger doesn't. But you'd better believe it's going in his belly!

And once it's in there—once Geeger's stomach is packed full of slimy, smelly, expired food— the robot plugs himself into his **DIGEST-O-TRON 5000**. The machine takes all the yucky stuff in Geeger's guts and—*vrroOoOM! Bzzt! WHOOSH!*—turns it into electricity.

LOTS of electricity.

One time, a storm knocked out the power in all of Amblerville. But Geeger was able to plug himself in and **provide** electricity to the whole entire town until a repair crew could fix the problem. He was a hero! Even the town newspaper, the *Amblerville Observer*, said so. They wrote a front-page article all about what Geeger did!

But Geeger isn't only good at his job. He's good at plenty of other things too. Like being a student.

That's right: Geeger goes to school! He attends Amblerville Elementary School, where he's in **Ms. Bork**'s class.

Geeger LOVES school. Every day, he wakes up eager to get there. He just can't wait to start learning and playing with his friends. There's **Tillie**, Geeger's best friend, plus a bunch of other fun and wonderful kids. Like **Arjun** and **Olivia** and **Mac** and **Sidney** and **Suzie** and **Gabe** and **Roxy** and **Raul**. And **Fudge**! That's Ms. Bork's class pet. A fuzzy, snuggly, adorable hamster.

But even though Geeger is excited to go to school every day, today he's more excited than ever. Because today, Geeger isn't even going to school. He and Ms. Bork

and all his classmates—but not
Fudge, unfortunately—are going
on a . . .

FIELD TRIP!

Instead of walking to school, like Geeger normally does, a school bus is going to come pick him up. And on that school bus will be all Geeger's classmates. They'll drive from one end of Amblerville to the other, all the way to the Amblerville History Museum. There, Geeger and his friends will learn all about their town, pausing only to do the thing that Geeger might be best at: **EAT! EAT! EAT! EAT! EAT!**

Except the cafeteria at the Amblerville History Museum doesn't serve

moldy, stale, expired, or rotten food.
And so, before the bus shows up at
his house, Geeger needs to pack
himself a lunch.

Get to it, Geeger!

2

BEEP! BEEP!

The first thing Geeger does is get his lunch box. But Geeger's lunch box is probably unlike any lunch box you've ever seen.

It's *enormous*, for one thing. It looks more like a suitcase

than a lunch box. And pack-
ing it can take a *looong* time.

Geeger sets his lunch box on the
counter. Flipping the clips that keep
it locked, he lifts the lid.

The instant the lunch box is
open, a scent comes **wafting** out
and quickly fills the kitchen. It's

the smell of expired beans and mushy bananas and moldy Brie cheese. You might not like it, but Geeger sure does. And as soon as the robot gets a whiff of it, his wires start buzzing and his brain tells him to **EAT!**

Geeger grabs a handful of soft, brownish-green oranges. He tosses one into his stomach, and drops the others into his lunch box.

Next, he reaches for a pile of slimy zucchinis. He sticks one into his mouth and is just about to dump the rest into his lunch box, when all of a sudden he hears:

HOOOOOONK!

It's a horn. The horn of a *vehicle*. And a *big* one, by the sound of it.

Maybe, Geeger thinks, *as big as a SCHOOL BUS.*

Tossing aside those slippery zucchinis, Geeger hurries to look out his window.

But there's no school bus outside.

The honk had come from a garbage truck. It does it again—*HOOOOOONK!*—trying to get a group of pigeons to hurry up and get out of the street.

Disappointed, Geeger gathers his zucchinis and sets them in his lunch box.

He's just about to reach for something that's either an extremely moldy hunk of cheese or an **exceptionally** old cantaloupe—it's hard to tell which one—when he hears:

Beeeeeep!

Geeger goes rushing back over to his window.

But there's *still* no school bus. Just

a minivan, honking at the garbage truck that's still—*HOOOOOONK!*—honking at those pigeons.

"BUM-mer," Geeger says.

But then, a beat later, he sees it. . . .

It's tall and yellow and rumbling around the corner onto Geeger's street.

A school bus.

Geeger gasps, the circuits inside him sparking with excitement.

And as if they were waiting for the school bus too, the pigeons finally take flight, clearing the way for the garbage truck and minivan to roll along.

The next thing Geeger knows, the bus—shining brightly in the sunlight—is right outside his house.

BEEP! BEEP! BEEEEEEP!

That's the bus, its horn sounding like a grown-up version of the minivan's baby beep. And Geeger knows that the bus is *BEEP! BEEP! BEEEEEEP*ing for *him*.

The robot quickly throws some more food into his lunch box, shuts the lid, latches the locks, then hurries out the door.

3

Secret Handshake

Geeger steps outside just as the windows of the school bus start sliding down. Then, one by one, Geeger's friends poke their heads out of the now-open spaces.

First Geeger sees Gabe, who's

sticking his tongue out and flaring his nostrils.

Then he sees Sidney, who gives Geeger a smile and a thumbs-up.

Next is Roxy, quickly followed by Olivia, Mac, Arjun, and Raul. They all wave and call for Geeger.

"Over here, Geeger!"

"Hey! Geeger!"

"Geeger! Check me out!"

Suzie sticks her head out next.

And then—last, but definitely not least—comes Tillie, Geeger's best friend in the whole galaxy. She gives the robot one of the grins that always makes the battery in his chest warm up. Then she says, "Happy Field Trip Day, Geeger! Come on! I saved you a seat!"

Geeger hears Tillie fine, but he doesn't go join her right away. Instead he spends a moment just standing there on his doorstep, looking at the school bus twinkling in the sun, trying to memorize the joyful expressions on every one of his friends' faces. It's a beautiful sight, and one Geeger hopes to never forget.

Then there's a sighing sound, and the bus suddenly sinks a few inches closer to the ground. It makes Geeger think of Tillie's dog, **Albert Einstein**—how he'll run around in zigzagging circles for an hour straight, then stop out of nowhere, give a big yawn, and plop down onto his belly. Geeger never really understood why Albert Einstein did that. But now, he's pretty sure he gets it. Sometimes you feel so excited, all you can do is run around in circles until you collapse.

A second later, the doors of the bus fold open. Then Ms. Bork appears, stepping out onto the street and planting her hands on her hips.

"Are you joining us, Geeger?" she asks.

"Are *yooou* KID-ding?" the robot

responds. "I would *nooot* MISS it for *theee* WORLD."

With that, Geeger wraps an arm around his lunch box. He hauls it across his lawn, and then follows Ms. Bork onto the bus.

"Good morning, my metal friend!" the robot hears as soon as he's made it aboard.

Geeger looks toward the voice, and sees a familiar face seated behind the bus's steering wheel. It's **Chef Mike**, the chef at Amblerville Elementary School. And he's holding something—a brown paper grocery bag with the words FOR GEEGER written on it in marker.

"I thought you might want a snack during our drive," Chef Mike says, handing the bag to Geeger.

And Geeger doesn't even need to open the thing up to know what's inside. His scent sensors can pick up the smell even through the thick, crinkly paper. Rotten eggs and spoiled avocado. And knowing how thoughtful Chef Mike is, he probably put a few slices of moldy bread in there too.

"THANK *yooou*," Geeger says,

taking the bag from Chef Mike.

"My pleasure," he says. Then he

hooks a thumb over his shoulder,

toward the rows of seats behind him. "Now get seated so I can get us to the museum."

Geeger goes, greeting each of his classmates as he does.

Gabe gets a fist bump.

Mac and Arjun and Olivia each get a wave.

Roxy and Raul get high fives.

Sidney gets a *"Heeey."*

Suzie gets a *"Hiii."*

And Tillie?

Tillie holds out her hand, and she and Geeger do their secret

handshake—which they only just finished perfecting a few days ago. It involves a fist bump, several slaps, a wiggling of the fingers, one snap, a wink, plus a shoulder roll, and it all happens so fast that no one else can possibly memorize it.

At the very end of it, both Tillie and Geeger giggle. That's not actually part of the secret handshake, but it happens every time anyway.

Finally, after tucking all his food under his seat, Geeger sits.

Up at the front of the bus, Chef Mike shouts, **"And we're OFF!"**

And with that, the school bus starts rumbling forward again.

4

Hiccup!

Geeger was right about one thing: being on a school bus with all your friends is FUN.

But there's one thing about the bus that Geeger hadn't expected . . .

It's BUMPY.

Very bumpy.

Geeger bops up and down and side to side the whole entire ride. He can feel his circuits sliding and his wires jangling. And in his stomach, the

BUMP-A BUMP-A BUMP!

moldy orange and rotten zucchini he had for breakfast keep bouncing and rolling around. But it's a good thing he's got *something* in there, because it's way too bumpy for him to eat the eggs and avocado Chef Mike gave him.

The bumpiness also makes it hard to have a conversation. But Geeger and Tillie can't help but talk. They're way too excited about the day ahead of them.

"Last night," Tillie says, "my dad and I—"

BUMP!

BUMP-A-BUMP BUMP!

Tillie waits for a pause in the bumping, then tries again:

"My dad and I—"

BA-BUMP!

"We went onto the museum's—"

BUMP!

"We went onto the museum's website. And guess what? They've got this **exhibit**. You won't believe it, Geeger. It's all about—"

BUMP-A-BUMP BA-BUMP BA-BUMP BA-BUMP BUMP!

Tillie hesitates, then opens her

mouth to finally get out what she's been trying to say. But instead of finishing her sentence, her eyes open wide, and she says, "Uh-oh."

"UH-*oooh*?" Geeger asks, confused. "The mu-SEUM has an EX-hib-it all A-bout UH-*oooh*?"

Tillie shakes her head.

"It's all about—*hiccup!*"

Hearing this, Geeger frowns. The robot has never been to a museum before. But Ms. Bork told him and his classmates what sorts of things they could expect to find at the

Amblerville History Museum, and an exhibit about hiccups definitely wasn't one of them.

"The mu-SEUM . . . ," Geeger says, as slowly and clearly as he can, ". . . has an EX-hib-it . . . all A-bout . . . HICC-up?"

Before Tillie can answer, Gabe— who's sitting across the aisle—calls over, "No! That big bump from a second ago—it gave her the—"

BA-BUMP!

"It gave her," Gabe begins again, "the—*hiccup!*"

Geeger blinks at Gabe. Now he's really confused.

Tillie says, "I—*hiccup!*"

Gabe says, "She just—*hiccup!*"

Then Olivia, who's sitting next to Gabe, sticks her head up and says, "Everyone's getting the—"

BUMP-A-BUMP-A-BUMP!

"*Hiccup!*" finishes Olivia.

A moment later, the bus rumbles to a stop at a red light. And now Geeger can hear them all around him:

"*Hic!*"

"*Hiccup!*"

"Hic!"

Hiccups, Geeger realizes. He's heard of them, but never seen them in action.

"Class?"

It's Ms. Bork. She's at the very front of the bus, standing up and facing them since the bus is stopped.

"We're just around the corner from the museum," she says. "When we get there, I want you to—*hiccup!*"

Ms. Bork claps a hand over her mouth.

Geeger grins.

"You WANT us *tooo* HICC-up?" he asks.

"That—*hiccup!*—shouldn't be—*hiccup!*—a problem," calls Gabe.

And in response, every other student on the bus lets out a hiccup of their own.

Even Geeger joins in. He doesn't actually have the hiccups—as far as he knows, robots can't get the hiccups—but he can pretend.

"HICC-UP!" he cries. **"HICC-HICC-HICC-UP!"**

At the front of the bus, Ms. Bork

lowers her hand from her mouth. And Geeger sees that her lips are turned up in a grin. But only for a second. Because then they open wide to let a gigantic laugh spill out.

Chef Mike turns around—the stoplight is still red. He looks at Ms. Bork, laughing even harder now, and then at all the kids, hiccupping behind him.

He says, "What in the world is going on in—"

But that's as far as he gets. His words are suddenly interrupted by a great big:

"HICCUP!"

And then everyone's not only hic-cupping, but laughing, too. Geeger laughs so hard that his circuits clang together.

The class hasn't even made it to the museum yet, and they're already having a blast. Right then, Geeger knows it: this day is sure to be one of the best of his life.

5

Museum Etiquette

Everyone manages to get rid of their hiccups by the time the bus pulls up to the Amblerville History Museum. Well, *almost* everyone.

As Ms. Bork once again stands up and turns around to address the

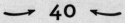

class, there are still a couple of stray hiccups to be heard here and there.

First one from Arjun.

Then one from Sidney.

Each one causes another round of giggles to spread throughout the school bus.

Ms. Bork waits for the laughter to peter out, then raises a hand to call for quiet.

"I know we're all excited," she says, keeping her voice low so that everyone has to really listen. "But it's important that we're on our

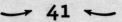

best behavior from here on out."

Ms. Bork then tells the class about something called *museum **etiquette***.

"That's just a fancy way of saying how you're supposed to behave inside the museum," she explains. "We need to speak quietly. We need to walk, not run. We need to be aware of those around us, and we need to be polite. We—"

Gabe raises his hand high.

"Yes, Gabe?" says Ms. Bork.

"What do we do if we get the hiccups?" he asks with a grin.

Ms. Bork smiles back at him.

"You make sure to hiccup as quietly as you can," she says. Then she points a finger out the window. "Now, as you can see, we're not the only classroom visiting the museum today."

Geeger looks where Ms. Bork is pointing. And there, parked in other spots in front of the museum, are other school buses. Geeger quickly counts six of them—and just as he's finishing, he sees a seventh pull in.

Each bus is big and yellow, exactly like the one Geeger is on. But the words printed along the sides of each bus are different. Geeger knows that his bus says AMBLERVILLE ELEMENTARY SCHOOL on it. Every other bus is stamped with the name of a different school.

Geeger wonders how many other kids there will be in the museum. Dozens, for sure. Maybe even hundreds. A thousand?

Ms. Bork, it seems, is thinking the same thing. "There will be lots of other kids in the museum with us today," she says. "It's essential that we stick together. No wandering off on your own. Make sure you can always see me. I'll be keeping track of all of *you*, of course. But there's only one of me, and there are—" Ms. Bork runs her eyes up and down the school bus's rows, counting her students. "*a whole bunch* of you," she finally says.

She takes a deep breath, like she's preparing herself for a difficult task ahead.

Then she says, "Okay, then. Who's ready to get inside?"

A few kids quietly raise their hands.

That's what Geeger does too.

The other kids all whisper, "*Me!*" or, "*I am!*" Ms. Bork gives the class a thumbs-up. "Excellent museum etiquette," she tells them.

Then she leads the way off the bus and up the wide stone steps at the front of the museum. At the top of the stairs, a woman in a fancy suit and a shiny name tag greets them with a smile, then pulls open a tall glass door.

Inside, seated behind a desk, is a man. He's got a suit and a name tag too, plus a little metal **contraption** in his hand. Geeger can't figure out what it is. Not until the man says, **"Stamps! Get your stamps!"**

One by one, Geeger's classmates hold out their hands to the man. And one by one, the man uses his little metal contraption to give them a stamp—a large star with the letters AHM in its center. At first, Geeger doesn't know what the letters mean. *AHM? Like* Um? he wonders. *Or* Ah? Geeger has learned that those are sounds people make when they're trying to figure out what to say. But why would a *star* be saying *um* or *ah*? Then, suddenly, Geeger realizes: he and his classmates are standing in the *Amblerville History Museum.* AHM!

When it's Geeger's turn to get his stamp, he holds his hand out to the man, just like his classmates did before him. But the man doesn't give him a stamp. Instead, he spends a second studying the robot's hand, then peers up at Geeger and grins.

And perhaps because Geeger doesn't know this man, he's not sure what to make of his grin. It's not like when Tillie or Ms. Bork aim one of *their* grins at him. When they do that, Geeger always knows it's a good thing, that they're either happy to see him or pleased with something he's done.

But this is different.

Geeger can't understand why this man is grinning at him like he is.

And what the man says next doesn't help clear up Geeger's confusion.

"Wait till you get in there!" he tells the robot.

And before Geeger can even think to ask him what he means, the man gives him a star stamp and says, **"Next!"**

6

Compost Piles

As soon as Geeger makes it a bit
farther into the museum, he for-
gets all about the stamp man and
that grin and those words that so
confused him. That's because the
museum is *fascinating*. There are

displays everywhere Geeger looks, and each one has a sign beside it that's absolutely packed with information.

One display is about all the different animal **species** that live in and around Amblerville. Next to it is a big glass case full of bones that had been found in the ground all over town, and next to *that* are a group of life-sized animal statues. There's a pair of deer, a fox, a few skunks, and a bunch of squirrels and chipmunks. Geeger finds it funny to imagine all those animals actually hanging out together.

Past the animal display, there's one detailing the kinds of foods that are best able to grow in Amblerville's soil. As part of this display, there's

a long table—even longer than the tables in the cafeteria of Geeger's school. And on the table? You guessed it. FOOD! Geeger sees several ears of corn. Little piles of red and black and brown beans. Bowls of cranberries and blueberries. Potatoes and carrots and cucumbers and peppers. And when Geeger gets closer, he sees that each item of food has a tiny sign of its own, full of information about how and when it grows. Geeger is amazed. He's always known that food is delicious, but it turns out it's interesting, too!

Geeger looks, then reads, then looks again and reads again. He can actually *feel* the wires that make up his brain **pulsing** with all the new facts he's filling them with. It makes him adore this little town he's come to call his own even more than he already did. All this, and Geeger's class has only made it through one of the museum's many rooms!

In the next room over, Geeger finds a display all about the Amblerville Diner, the oldest of the

restaurants in town. There's another big glass case beside this one, and Geeger can hardly believe what he discovers inside it. His lunch! At least that's what it looks like. It's a heap of rotten fruit and vegetables— Geeger identifies some of the beans and berries from the table in the previous room—all of it mixed up with what appears to be coffee grounds and dirt. This is, Geeger learns, a compost pile: a collection of food waste that can be used to help new food grow.

Old, unwanted food being turned into energy?

It sounds a lot like Geeger!

The robot is amazed. He wants to know everything he can about compost piles. And he has *so* many questions!

Is there anything you *can't* put in one of the piles? How long does it take before you can use compost to grow something new? What does a compost pile *smell* like? Are there compost piles everywhere? How big can one be?

Behind him, Geeger can hear Ms. Bork.

"All right," she's saying. "Is everyone ready?"

The class is moving on to another room. And Geeger knows he's supposed to go with them. But he's not done learning about compost piles yet. He hasn't even finished reading the sign! He has to do *that*. It will only take a second. Then he'll go and rejoin his friends. That'll be fine, right?

Right, Geeger tells himself.

But instead of a second, it takes him several minutes to finish up with the compost pile display. And when he finally turns around, Ms. Bork and his classmates are nowhere to be found.

"UH-*oooh*."

7

Lost

The battery in Geeger's chest warms up.

Then it goes cold.

And then it warms up again.

The robot is in a full-fledged PANIC.

Because he can't see Ms. Bork. And he can't see any of his friends, either.

He's *lost*.

And while Geeger now knows all about how to start and sustain a compost pile, none of that information is going to help him find his class.

Geeger looks around the room. There are four walls. Three of them have one doorway. The fourth has *two*. That's five different ways that Ms. Bork and his classmates could've gone!

Where should he look first?

Or should he not look at all?

Should he stay right where he is and wait for Ms. Bork to notice he's gone and come look for him?

Geeger is trying to make up his mind one way or the other when he hears something that distracts him from his **predicament**.

"Is that a—no way."

"What is that thing doing here?"

Geeger turns toward the voices. Across the room, he sees a group

of kids. They're older than Geeger's classmates, and all of them are frowning—and frowning at *him*.

"Whoa," says one of the kids as soon as Geeger's eyes land on them. "Can it *hear* us?"

"It's so creepy!" says another.

The rest of the kids laugh.

Then one of the kids' frowns flips into a grin. And a grin that Geeger has no trouble reading. He knows it doesn't mean anything good.

Then one of the others says, "Do you think it knows it's supposed to *rain* later? Bye-bye, robot. Hello, *rust*-bot."

They all laugh again.

And Geeger?

Geeger just stares at them, stunned and confused and hurt. He no longer feels like finding Ms. Bork and his classmates. What he feels like doing is leaving the museum— running right back out that tall glass door, then down those wide stone steps, all the way through Amblerville, and out of town.

But before Geeger can take a single step in *any* direction, he feels a hand on his shoulder. He turns and sees a familiar face. It's the man from before—the one from behind the desk, who'd given Geeger his star stamp, grinned at him, and said, *Wait till you get in there.* Is this what

he had meant? Had the man some-
how known these kids would be
here, and that they'd say these mean
things about Geeger? Did the man
feel the same way about the robot?
Did *everyone* think of Geeger like
that?

"Come on," says the stamp man,
steering Geeger across the room and
through one of the five doorways.

Geeger's not sure where the man
is taking him. But he wouldn't be the
least bit surprised if it was outside—
into the rain to rust.

8

Amblerville's Bots

"Voila!"

It's the stamp man who says
it. He does so right after leading
Geeger through another doorway,
then sweeping an arm out to his
side with a dramatic **flourish**.

Geeger looks—and sees Ms. Bork, and then all his classmates. There's Arjun and Olivia. There's Sidney and Mac and Suzie. There's Gabe and Roxy and Raul. And there's Tillie, giving the robot her biggest, very best grin—the one that never fails to cheer Geeger up. But just now, after the incident in the other room, even the sight of his best friend in the galaxy isn't working its magic on Geeger. He still feels uncomfortable, unwelcome, and unwanted.

Until the stamp man says, "So what do you think?"

"WHAT do I *thiiink*?" Geeger asks.

The man jerks his chin at something over the robot's head.

Geeger turns around and sees a sign hanging over the doorway. It's similar to the ones in all the other rooms, there to let the museum's visitors know what they can expect to find in that space's displays and cases.

This sign, though, doesn't say

Amblerville's Origins or Amblerville's Animals or Amblerville's
Industry. It says AMBLERVILLE'S BOTS.

It's only then, once he's read that
word—*bots*—that Geeger notices
what's in all the displays and
cases surrounding him. *Robots,* of

course. Robots just like him.

The stamp man grins. And this time, Geeger has no doubt about it—it's one of the *good* kinds.

"Go ahead," he tells the robot. "Take a look."

Geeger takes a tour of the room. He studies each display and the contents of each case. He reads every sign. And he discovers that robots have been a part of Amblerville since its very beginning.

Soon after it became a town, a resident built a bot to help sweep the streets. And the bot is right there, safe inside a glass case. Its sides are a bit dented, and the broom it clutches in one hand barely has any bristles left. But it still works! There's a sign that says so, and that has an arrow pointing to a big yellow button. Geeger presses it—and the bot begins to sweep, lowering the broom and swishing it back and forth.

Not long after that bot was built, someone else created an ice-cream-scooping bot. It worked at the general store alongside teenagers and adults. This bot had a light bulb on top of its head—**just like Geeger!**—and not two, or even four, but *six* arms, each one equipped with an ice-cream scoop.

A little while after *that* bot was built, someone made one to help

direct traffic during Amblerville's annual summer parade. This bot had a speaker in its chest and could make its voice boom loud enough to

MEET GEEGER

be heard from several blocks away. According to a sign Geeger reads, the bot would call out warnings and directions—but also sometimes *sing*.

Finally, in the room's very last display, Geeger sees . . .

. . . *himself.*

MEET GEEGER, the sign on the display says, and along with it are dozens of pictures. One shows the scientists who designed, built, and programmed Geeger. Another shows Geeger eating his first meal (a pile of mushy brown bananas, expired garbanzo beans, and moldy whole wheat bread). Another shows Geeger plugging himself into his DIGEST-O-TRON 5000. Another shows him

and the machine helping provide electricity to the town after a storm knocked out all the power. And yet another shows Geeger at Amblerville Elementary School, standing on the playground, smiling alongside Ms. Bork and all his classmates.

Seeing all this, Geeger couldn't feel more different from how he did just a few minutes ago. He feels the exact opposite of unwelcome and unwanted.

He gazes at the picture of his class on the playground. He finds his own face among all the other faces, and sees Tillie's right beside his.

And then she's right there, actually standing beside him in the museum, the ends of her curly hair touching his elbow.

Robots don't hiccup. They also don't cry. Not when they're sad, and not when they're happy, either. But here's what *does* happen when a robot like Geeger feels how he does in that moment. The batteries in their chests warm up to the coziest of temperatures, and a gentle, sparkly energy courses through their wires. Their circuits sizzle the slightest bit, and the light bulbs atop their heads hum with a soft, yellow glow.

Standing there in the museum, feeling that feeling, Geeger closes his eyes.

Until he hears some kids laughing behind him.

"Oooh, look who it is," one of them says. "The *rust*-bot."

Geeger doesn't have to turn around to know that it's those same older kids from before. But their words don't bother him like they did earlier.

He turns around and gives the kids a nice wave and a big, proud smile. After all, he's *Geeger*—one of Amblerville's bots.

Word List

contraption (con•TRAP•shun): A machine or device; a gadget

etiquette (EH•tih•ket): The way you're supposed to behave in a certain place or at a certain time

exceptionally (eks•SEP•shun•uh•lee): To a greater degree than normal

exhibit (eks•ZIB•it): A public display of a work of art or something else of interest

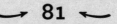

flourish (FLUH•rish): A bold gesture or action

predicament (preh•DIK•a•ment): A difficult situation

provide (pruh•VYDE): Make available for use

pulsing (PUHL•sing): A rhythmic throbbing or vibration

species (SPEE•shees): A kind of animal or plant

wafting (WAF•ting): Passing gently through the air

Questions

1. Have you ever gone on a field trip? Where did you go? Did you enjoy it?

2. Geeger and Tillie have their very own secret handshake. Have you ever had a secret handshake with someone? Could you invent one?

3. Is there a museum near where you live? Have you been to it? What sort of displays did it have?

4. In Chapter 5, Geeger realizes that the letters AHM stand for Amblerville History Museum.

This sort of abbreviation is called an *acronym*. Do you know any other acronyms?

5. In Chapter 7, Geeger feels very out of place, and like he doesn't belong. Have you ever felt like that? When? Where? Did something happen to make you feel better?

6. In the final chapter, Geeger finds a display about himself in the museum! Would you ever want to be in a museum like that? What kind of a museum? What would you be celebrated for?